… SHARKS

BULL SHARK

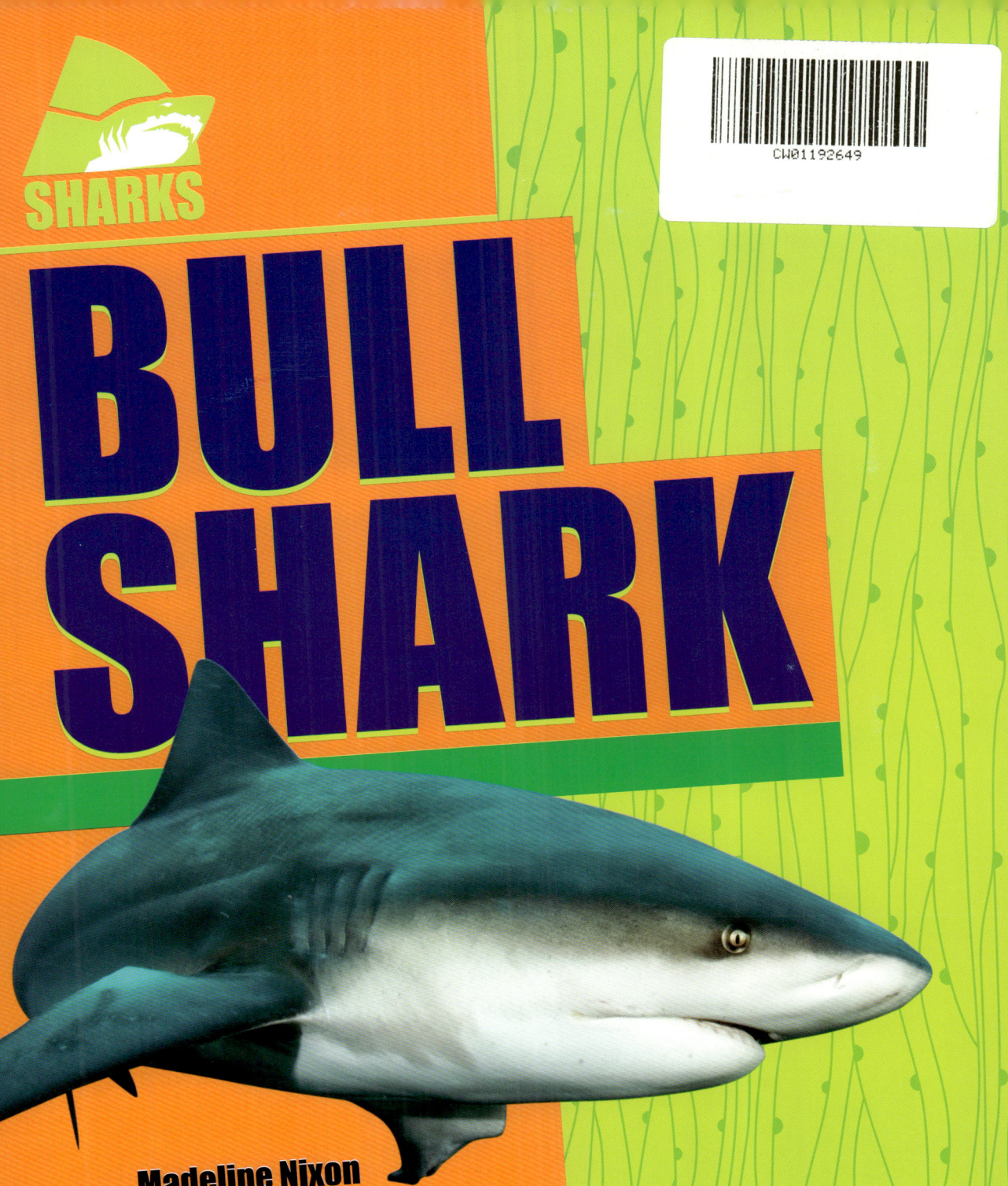

Madeline Nixon

AV2
www.av2books.com

Step 1
Go to www.av2books.com

Step 2
Enter this unique code

VNPWSP473

Step 3
Explore your interactive eBook!

CONTENTS
- 2 AV2 Book Code
- 4 What Is a Bull Shark?
- 6 Bull Shark Features
- 8 Bull Shark Life Cycle
- 10 Life in the Ocean
- 12 Bull Sharks around the World
- 14 Finding Food
- 16 Bull Shark History
- 18 People and Bull Sharks
- 20 Protecting Bull Sharks
- 22 Test Your Knowledge
- 23 Key Words

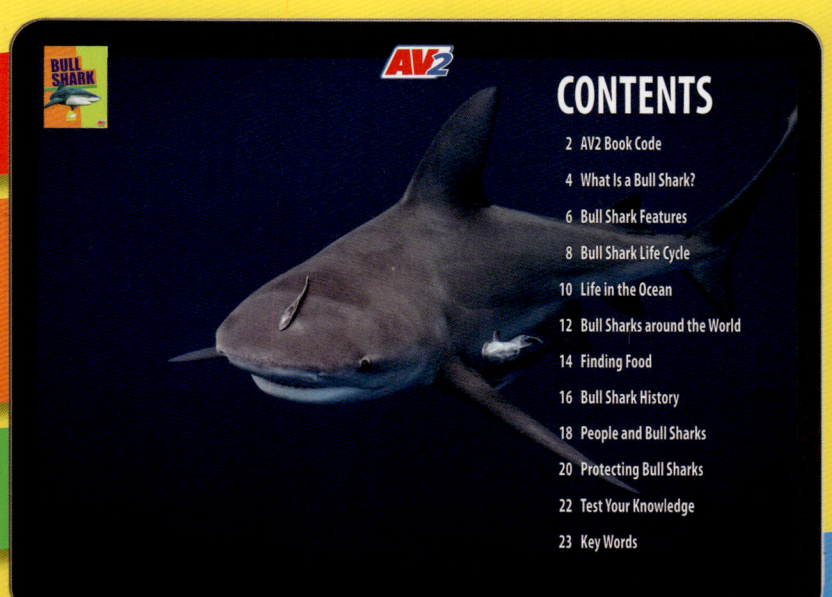

AV2 is optimized for use on any device

Your interactive eBook comes with...

Contents
Browse a live contents page to easily navigate through resources

Audio
Listen to sections of the book read aloud

Videos
Watch informative video clips

Weblinks
Gain additional information for research

Try This!
Complete activities and hands-on experiments

Key Words
Study vocabulary, and complete a matching word activity

Quizzes
Test your knowledge

Slideshows
View images and captions

... and much, much more!

View new titles and product videos at www.av2books.com

BULL SHARK

CONTENTS

- 2   AV2 Book Code
- 4   What Is a Bull Shark?
- 6   Bull Shark Features
- 8   Bull Shark Life Cycle
- 10   Life in the Ocean
- 12   Bull Sharks around the World
- 14   Finding Food
- 16   Bull Shark History
- 18   People and Bull Sharks
- 20   Protecting Bull Sharks
- 22   Test Your Knowledge
- 23   Key Words/Index

What Is a Bull Shark?

There are more than 500 types of sharks. Just like humans, they come in many different sizes and shapes. Bull sharks get their name from their big bodies and fierce behavior. Like bulls, they head-butt their victims when they attack. Bull sharks are not the largest sharks, but they are some of the most dangerous.

"Bull sharks inhabit quite shallow waters, which means that they do have a great opportunity to interact with humans."

—George Burgess, curator of the International Shark Attack File at the Florida Museum of Natural History

Bull Shark

Scientific Name *Carcharhinus leucas*
Diet Carnivore
Size 7–11.5 feet (2.1–3.5 meters)
Weight 200–500 pounds (91–227 kilograms)
Conservation Status Near threatened
Population Unknown

Bull Shark 5

Bull Shark Features

Bull sharks have features that help them live. Some help them to hunt. Others help them to stay alive.

Body
A bull shark can control the amount of salt in its body's water. This allows it to live in both **fresh water** and salt water.

Shape
A bull shark's body is short and tough. This helps it move quickly and strike easily.

Snout
A bull shark's snout is round and wide. This helps it bump and surprise prey when it attacks.

Bull Shark

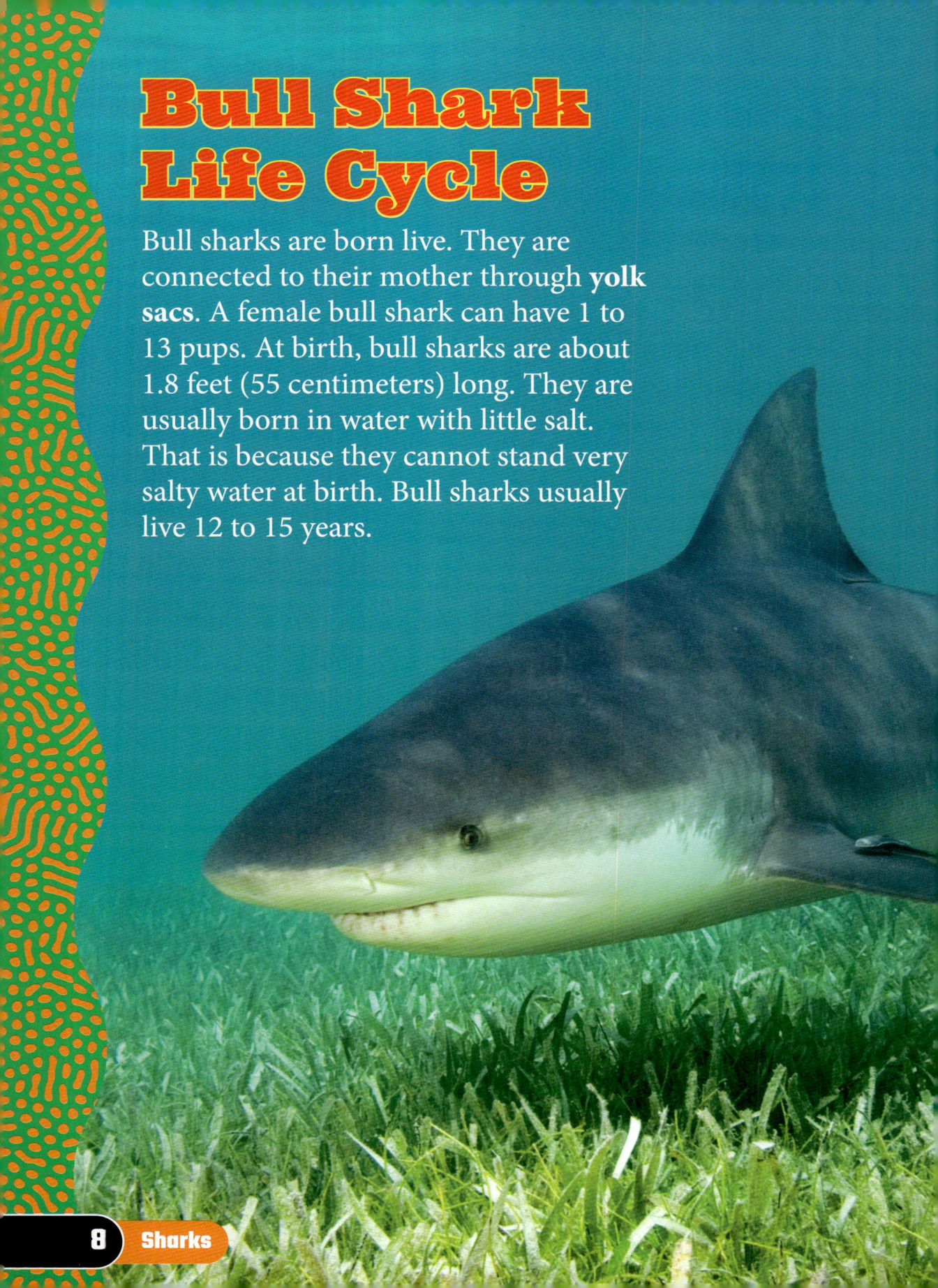

Bull Shark Life Cycle

Bull sharks are born live. They are connected to their mother through **yolk sacs**. A female bull shark can have 1 to 13 pups. At birth, bull sharks are about 1.8 feet (55 centimeters) long. They are usually born in water with little salt. That is because they cannot stand very salty water at birth. Bull sharks usually live 12 to 15 years.

How Big Are Sharks?

Human
5.5 feet (1.7 m)

Blacktip Shark
8 feet (2.4 m)

Bull Shark
11.5 feet (3.5 m)

Shortfin Mako Shark
12 feet (3.7 m)

Tiger Shark
16 feet (4.9 m)

Great Hammerhead Shark
20 feet (6.1 m)

Great White Shark
20 feet (6.1 m)

Whale Shark
32 feet (9.8 m)

Bull Shark

Life in the Ocean

Bull sharks usually live in warm, shallow waters. They have also been seen in rivers and lakes. They are some of the only sharks that can live in both fresh and salt water. Bull sharks have been spotted jumping rapids like salmon to swim **upstream**. They live in areas where there are a lot of people. Bull sharks will eat almost anything they find.

SHARK BITES

Bull sharks can sometimes be found in waters as deep as **492 feet** (150 m).

Bull Shark

Bull Sharks around the World

Bull sharks can be found around the world. They usually live in **coastal** waters. Bull sharks need warm water. They do not live around Europe, Canada, or Antarctica.

LEGEND ■ Bull Shark Range   ■ Land   ■ Water

1. Lake Nicaragua, Nicaragua

Many bull sharks live in Lake Nicaragua, a freshwater lake. At first, scientists believed it was a different shark **species**. Then, they learned that bull sharks could live in fresh water, too.

2. Florida, United States of America

Bull sharks are some of the most common sharks found along Florida's coastlines.

3. Carbrook Golf Club, Brisbane, Australia

During the 1990s, Australia's Logan River flooded. It trapped a group of bull sharks in a lake at the Carbrook Golf Club. The lake has many fish for them to eat. The bull sharks are still there today.

PACIFIC OCEAN

AUSTRALIA

Bull Shark 13

Finding Food

Bull sharks hunt alone. They are **carnivores**. That means they usually eat only meat. Bull sharks eat everything from fish to birds, turtles, and **marine mammals**. They even eat other bull sharks. Bull sharks have very strong jaws. They can bite through shells, skin, and scales.

SHARK BITES

The **story *Jaws*** was based on **shark attacks** that happened in **1916** in New Jersey. Bull sharks were **blamed** for these **attacks**.

Bull Shark 15

Bull Shark History

Achille Valenciennes, a French **zoologist**, discovered bull sharks in 1839. They have different names around the world. In Africa, they are known as "Zambezi sharks," after a river. People have discovered bull sharks in many different places. About 500 bull sharks live in the Brisbane River in Australia. Some have even been found in the Mississippi River.

A bull shark was once found in the Amazon River, about 2,500 miles (4,023 km) from the ocean.

Bull Shark 17

People and Bull Sharks

Bull sharks are known as the most dangerous sharks in the world. Mostly, they bite people when they are curious. However, the reason for some attacks is unknown. Their powerful jaws and teeth can injure or kill in one bite. Bull sharks like murky water. Swimming in clear water is a good way to avoid bites.

Bull sharks do well in **captivity**. They are the most popular shark to have in aquariums.

SHARK BITES

Bull sharks have attacked **hundreds** of people since **1580**.

Bull Shark 19

Protecting Bull Sharks

Humans hunt bull sharks for their meat and **fins**. Since there are many bull sharks by the shore, fishers sometimes catch them instead of other fish. There are no laws protecting bull sharks. They can be hunted freely.

Bull sharks are shrinking in length. There are not as many older sharks. This could mean that their numbers are dropping.

The bull shark became near threatened in 2005. This is a drop from least concern in 2000.

Bull Shark Conservation Status

EX	EW	CR	EN	VU	NT	LC
Extinct	Extinct in the Wild	Critically Endangered	Endangered	Vulnerable	Near Threatened	Least Concern

Bull Shark 21

Test Your Knowledge

1 Is the bull shark considered the most dangerous shark?

Yes

2 How do bull sharks survive in both salt water and fresh water?

They can control the amount of salt in their body

3 How deep can bull sharks be found?

492 feet (150 m)

4 Who discovered the bull shark and when?

Achille Valenciennes, 1839

5 What do bull sharks mainly eat?

Fish, birds, turtles, marine mammals

6 Why does Carbrook Golf Course have bull sharks in its lake?

Logan River flooded in the 1990s

7 What do bull sharks have in common with salmon?

They jump rapids to swim upstream

8 How did bull sharks get their name?

From their bodies and behavior

22 Sharks

Key Words

captivity: when an animal is in a zoo or aquarium

carnivores: animals that eat meat

coastal: near the shore

fins: the thin parts of a fish's body that help it swim

fresh water: water that has no salt

marine mammals: mammals that live in or near water, such as walruses, whales, and seals

species: a group of closely related animals

upstream: in the opposite direction that water is flowing

yolk sacs: gooey layers surrounding babies before birth

zoologist: a person who studies the animal kingdom

Index

age 8
aquariums 18
attack 4, 5, 7, 15, 18, 19

body 6, 7, 22

carnivores 5, 14
conservation status 5, 21

features 6, 7
food 10, 13, 14, 22
fresh water 6, 10, 13, 22

history 16, 17
humans 4, 5, 9, 10, 16, 18, 19, 20

life cycle 8, 9

population 5, 20
prey 7

salt water 6, 8, 10, 22
skin 14
snout 7

teeth 18

warm waters 10, 12
weight 5

Bull Shark 23

Get the best of both worlds.

AV2 bridges the gap between print and digital.

The expandable resources toolbar enables quick access to content including **videos**, **audio**, **activities**, **weblinks**, **slideshows**, **quizzes**, and **key words**.

Animated videos make static images come alive.

Resource icons on each page help readers to further **explore key concepts**.

Published by AV2
350 5th Avenue, 59th Floor
New York, NY 10118
Website: www.av2books.com

Copyright © 2021 AV2
All rights reserved. No part of this publication may be reproduced, stored in a retrieval system, or transmitted in any form or by any means, electronic, mechanical, photocopying, recording, or otherwise, without the prior written permission of the publisher.

Library of Congress Control Number: 2019955131

ISBN 978-1-7911-2115-0 (hardcover)
ISBN 978-1-7911-2116-7 (softcover)
ISBN 978-1-7911-2117-4 (multi-user eBook)
ISBN 978-1-7911-2118-1 (single-user eBook)

Printed in Guangzhou, China
1 2 3 4 5 6 7 8 9 0   24 23 22 21 20

022020
101119

Project Coordinator: John Willis
Designer: Terry Paulhus

Every reasonable effort has been made to trace ownership and to obtain permission to reprint copyright material. The publishers would be pleased to have any errors or omissions brought to their attention so that they may be corrected in subsequent printings.

AV2 acknowledges Alamy, Getty Images, iStock, Minden Pictures, and Shutterstock as its primary image suppliers for this title.

View new titles and product videos at www.av2books.com